Acknowledge

My heartfelt thanks goes to my co-conspirator
Sian Evans who brought this book to life with
her amazing illustrations. Without her,
Captain Celery would not have sailed.

Thanks also goes to the teachers and children
of Bishopsgate School who allowed me to
test run Captain Celery on World Book Day.

Of course, my children Milo and Ella were my
fiercest critics, but I thank them for their honesty.

My gratitude also goes to my wife
Gabby who made it all happen and to
Tessa Hewitt who designed the book.

And finally, appreciation for that wonderful
vegetable celery which inspired this tale.

For Milo and Ella

ISBN: 9798639680649

Contents

Two Very Different Pirates

One of the best jobs you could get 400 years ago was being a pirate, even though it was pretty much the most dangerous thing you could do.

Pirates had a lot of adventures and stole lots of money, but sadly very few grew old. Most ended up on the bottom of the sea.

Here's a tale about two pirates – one who ended up at the bottom of the sea and the other who grew to be very old.

Captain Firebeard

Pirate number one is Captain Samuel Lawrence Firebeard who got his name after setting his own beard on fire to show off how tough he was.

He had a glass eye, a metal hook for a hand and a wooden leg. In fact, most parts of his body were either damaged or missing.

Firebeard was, without question, the most fearsome pirate in the land. He was as big as a bear, as strong as an ox and would rather have a good fight than a good chat.

Captain Firebeard loved adventure and had sailed the world in search of treasure and excitement. He had fought in the seas of America, Africa and Australia and stolen lots of money which he never spent. One day he would stop being a pirate and treat himself to a new leg, but that day was not today.. nor tomorrow.

Captain Celery

Pirate number two was nothing like number one. He was half the size, and twice as clever.

Meet Captain Horatio Celery, a lean, nimble and happy stick of a man, named after his favourite vegetable.

Captain Celery was playful and full of fun, but he was no softy. He had won many battles and helped himself to a fair bit of gold, but not once had he hurt anyone. His main weapon was his big brain which he used with great skill to cheat and trick people into parting with their treasure.

It was plain for all to see that Celery and Firebeard had nothing in common even though they were both pirates.

This story is about how their paths crossed with disastrous consequences for one of them.

A Cunning Plan

It's the year 1662 in the Port of Bristol. Everyone is busy. Loading boats, unloading boats. Drinking rum and having fun.

Up a narrow, cobbled street, in a dark and pongy pub, a group of pirates was deep in a conversation which soon turned into an argument, and then into a fight.

"I will go on me own then," snarled Captain Firebeard as he withdrew his hook from a poor pirate's eye socket.

Firebeard was fuming because no-one liked his daring plan to attack a ship laden with gold and bring the shining coins and glittering necklaces all the way back from the far away islands of the Caribbean to Bristol.

Although he hated other pirates, he needed another ship to help him carry all the treasure home.

Whilst attracted by the thought of riches beyond their dreams, the lesser pirates in the room were scared. Frightened of sailing 4,000 miles across the rough waters of the Atlantic Ocean, frightened of fighting a heavily guarded ship belonging to the King of Spain and, most of all, frightened of Firebeard.

Firebeard huffed, puffed and swallowed the last drop of rum, slammed down his tankard and headed for the door.

"I'll come with you." A small, shrill voice pierced the smoky darkness of the pub.

The room went silent. The smokers stopped puffing. The drinkers stopped drinking. And Firebeard stopped going.

It was pirate number two – Captain Horatio Celery.
Firebeard turned to face Celery and sneered.

"You? A fat lot of good you'd be with those skinny
arms and stick legs."

Celery leapt up on to a table in a single bound,
pulled out Firebeard's sword and threw it like a
giant dart at the wall where it stuck fast.

"I am fighting fit and fit to fight," shrilled Celery.
Firebeard was flabbergasted. Stunned by Celery's
agility and nerve.

"Humph. You got a name, Pirate?", quizzed
Firebeard.

"Celery, Captain Celery."

"Well, stick man, we sail at dawn. Be thcre."

With those words, Firebeard retrieved his sword
and limped towards the door. Tomorrow beckoned.

Setting Sail

An orange sun rose over Bristol docks bathing the sails of Captain Firebeard's ship – the Black Oyster – in a warm light. Firebeard stirred in his hammock and let out the mightiest fart which woke the entire crew.

"Take on the provisions and prepare to set sail," bellowed Firebeard.

His crew leapt out of bed, pulled on their trousers and made their way up on deck to ready the ship for sail.

Mr Crabb, named on account of his love of raw crustaceans, was the ship quartermaster, meaning he was in charge of loading provisions for the voyage.

Standing on the gang plank with paper and pencil, he ticked off his purchases.

150 flagons of rum
20 sides of salted pig
35 live chickens
5 bushels of dried peas
12 pecks of pepper
15 cases of ship's biscuits
5 quarts of pickled fish heads
Three score of cannon balls
A live goat
More rum
A barrel of gunpowder
Rum

Firebeard suddenly remembered that the stick man was sailing with him to help steal the gold.

Where is that wisp of a man, he thought as he climbed the steps to the quarterdeck.

Across the harbour, he spotted Celery's ship
– the Happy Goose – with its bright green sails.
Like him, Celery was taking on stores for the
long, perilous journey.

150 flagons of water
5 tons of potatoes
5 bushels of carrots
A sack of quinoa
10 crates of fresh apples
A peck of saffron

Firebeard boomed across the water:
"You'll not get far on rabbit food, Celery."

Celery stopped loading his goods, smiled and
retorted: "I have been to Spain on an avocado, to
the Americas on an artichoke and to deepest Africa
on no more than a chickpea."

Firebeard huffed and shouted: "All hands on deck – prepare to cast off."

His crew swarmed the deck like ants, climbing rigging, lashing down barrels and untying the heavy ropes that kept the ship against the dock.

A light breeze caught the mainsail and the Black Oyster glided down the river towards the sea.

Behind them, the green sails of the Happy Goose propelled the ship forward through the water.

Ahead of them lay a six-week voyage through violent storms and dead calm seas. They would see giant whales blowing fountains of water high in the air;  flying fish gliding over the deck and schools of dolphins would race them through the waves.

That night, Firebeard was disturbed by his least favourite sound – laughter.

It's Not Funny

Having fun was something Firebeard did not approve of. He had no experience of fun and treated it with great suspicion.

So, when the burble of laughter bounced across the water from The Happy Goose, Firebeard went crazy.

"Silence, ye jabbering scallywags!"

The laughter got louder.

"Quiet, ye lily-livered scurvy dogs!"

The guffaws subsided into snorts, then titters, chuckles, chortles then silence.

Peace at last for Firebeard – until the next night, then the next and following nights. In fact, every night for the next 42 days, The Happy Goose shook with laughter and Firebeard shook with rage.

Then it got worse. Firebeard's own crew started laughing. They couldn't help it. It was infectious.

Young Tommy Benbow was the first to be punished. Firebeard sewed his mouth up with a needle and thread and tied him to the mast as a warning to anyone else thinking of laughing.

The Black Oyster fell silent and miserable again. Days 2 to 41 passed without pain. Celery kept the Happy Goose a mile down wind so as not to irritate Firebeard with all the sounds of fun. Tommy Benbow was not having fun – unable to eat or drink, he died.

On day 42, a voice screamed out from high up in the crow's nest. "Land ahoy!"

The two Captains reached for their telescopes and scanned the horizon for land. Sure enough, there it was. The island of St Kitts – a shimmering jewel in the Caribbean Sea.

Both captains did something they never normally do. Celery stopped laughing and Firebeard smiled.

42 days of salted pork, dry beans and rum was over.

They had arrived.

Gold Galore

Firebeard manoeuvred his ship up against the Happy Goose and dropped anchor. For the first time in six weeks the crews of the two pirate ships met face to face. It was an odd sight – the slim muscular frames of Celery's men next to the fat, contorted bodies from the Black Oyster.

"Let's fight!" yelled Firebeard's toothless first mate.

"Let's dance!" replied a sailor from the Happy Goose.

"Now, listen up," roared Firebeard. "The only fighting you'll be doing is fighting to stay alive…

…and the only dancing will be me on your grave!"

Firebeard gestured for the men to gather round as he explained his plan.

Tomorrow morning just after the sun rose, the Spanish Galleon El Cortes would pass through the narrow straights between St Kitts and the tiny island of Nevis.

El Cortes would be laden with gold and only lightly defended with four cannons and a handful of the king's soldiers.

The Happy Goose would lie in wait off Turtle Beach and when El Cortes was in sight, swiftly cut across her bow.

El Cortes would turn and run towards Nevis where the Black Oyster would be waiting ready to attack. That was the plan. What could go wrong?

That night all was quiet on board the two ships, save for the odd snore and pirate fart.

As the sun appeared over the horizon, Firebeard ordered the crew to ready themselves for battle. The Happy Goose was all rigged and ready.

Then at about 7 am, the Spanish Treasure Ship glided into view. She sat low in the water, listing to one side with the weight of gold.

Captain Celery gave a shrill whistle and the crew heaved in the sails to catch the wind. The Happy Goose lurched forward cutting through the water at a terrific rate. Celery stood at the wheel with a broad grin on his face as the wind caught the curls in his hair.

The Happy Goose was bearing down on the El Cortes so quickly that no-one on board had time to react.

Quick as a flash, Celery's ship cut across the bow of the Spanish galleon spraying its deck with the foaming droplets of saltwater.

The El Cortes jibed to the portside, sending barrels, men and chests of gold coins sliding across the deck in a noisy tangle of metal and flesh.

Captain Firebeard watched in amazement and pleasure as he steered his ship towards the stricken vessel.

"Attack!," he screamed at the top of his voice, which was very loud and very frightening.

He brought the Black Oyster alongside El Cortes with a thump and dozens of his mangy men leapt aboard waving their swords overhead.

With a swoosh and groan, Firebeard's pirates hacked down the Spanish sailors. Not a man was spared. Even the captain was slaughtered and thrown into the Caribbean without so much as a goodbye.

The battle over, Firebeard 's one healthy eye scanned the horizon. Where was Celery? He was meant to be helping…

"Celery, you weasel. Blistering barnacles, where are you man?" he bellowed.

Firebeard grew red in the face, puffed up like a puffer fish – then deflated like a burst balloon. He'd had a thought. Celery's absence was actually good news.

"You run and hide, Celery. The treasure is now all mine. Every single coin, every jewel, everything is mine."

The crew laughed and began the back-breaking task of loading the treasure on board the Black Oyster. There were oak chests brimming with gold coins, sacks full of jewellery and barrels stuffed with precious stones.

No one had seen so much treasure. It was beyond imagination.

After two hours in the blistering Caribbean sun, the first mate shouted out to Captain Firebeard.

"It 'aint gonna fit Capt'n. There's too much."

The Black Oyster was sitting very low in the water as the weight of the treasure pressed her downwards.

Firebeard was swift to reply to the worried first mate: "Strip the boat of everything apart from her sails."

"But we'ze gonna need our provisions Capt'n. We need food, water and gunpowder for the journey home," he pleaded.

But Firebeard was determined not leave a single coin behind. Everything was thrown overboard. The beds, the pots, the pans, the food, the water, the guns.

Every inch of the ship was stripped bare to make way for more gold.

The Black Oyster wallowed in the water like a fat wooden hippo.

As the last glimmering coin was loaded, Firebeard ordered the crew to set sail for home.

The Black Oyster creaked and groaned as the wind caught her sails. Slowly, very slowly she got underway to start the six-week voyage back to England.

Green Treasure

So what had happened to Celery? Why had he sailed all this way not to collect his reward?

Well, the night before Celery had spotted something more valuable to him than any gold.

He'd seen huge swathes of green foliage wrapped around the hillside of the island of Nevis.

He knew that colour. It was celery, growing tall and strong under the Caribbean sunshine. Acres of it.

Once Firebeard was out of sight, Celery sailed to Nevis and launched his rowing boats.

Each boat carried four men armed with swords.

The men moved like locusts through the celery, harvesting the lush green crop. They made several return trips to the island until every stick was cut and loaded onto the Happy Goose.

Unlike gold, celery is not very heavy so, despite being full to the brim, the Happy Goose did not sink low in the water.

Delighted with their haul, the crew of the Happy Goose began to dance a strange dance knocking sticks of celery together as they lept in the air chanting "Celery, Celery."

"Let's head for home lads, "cried Captain Celery and the Happy Goose weighed anchor and darted off in the direction of Bristol.

Fools Gold

Two days into the voyage, Captain Firebeard knew he was in for trouble. With no food and water, his men were getting tetchy. Most had already developed a disease known as scurvy which you get if you don't eat fruit and vegetables.

Ask any pirate about scurvy and you will hear about teeth falling out, terrible diarrhoea and limbs that have rotted away.

The men that weren't ill were drunk so Captain Firebeard had to sail his fat ship alone.

On day 14, Firebeard ordered that the fattest man be captured and boiled up for supper.

Poor old Tommy Butter, the ship's cook, paid the price for sneaking extra food onto his plate.

It was not a good taste, but the crew were grateful to Tommy.

On day 25, the sky darkened over and the winds picked up. A storm was brewing. This was very, very bad news for the Black Oyster. Overloaded with gold, even small waves broke over the deck swamping the ship.

Firebeard ordered Dan, a young deck hand, to climb to the crow's nest to look for land. The skinny, starving boy clambered to the top of the mast and scanned the horizon with a telescope.

The other thing about scurvy is that it makes you go half blind and Dan had real trouble seeing straight. He thought he saw land, but it was a seagull. Then he saw a great grey lump. Was that land?

Yes, it had to be.

"Land ahoy, Captain!" he feebly cried.

"Due west, sir"

Firebeard hauled the wheel round and headed in the direction of the lump.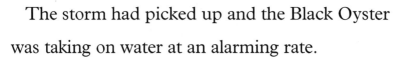

The storm had picked up and the Black Oyster was taking on water at an alarming rate. The skies were so dark that Firebeard did not see the grey lump until his ship hit it.

It wasn't a crash. There was no sound of wood splintering on rock. It was more of a thud, like a punch.

Firebeard and Dan were hurled forward and landed with a squelch on the back of a giant whale.

The whale waved its massive tail which came crashing down on the Black Oyster smashing it to tiny pieces.

Flashes of gold filled the black skies as the treasure was scattered across the waves.

Firebeard groaned in despair as the Black Oyster sank to the bottom of the ocean with all its treasure.

He stuck his hook deep into the whale's blubber and hauled himself to the top of beast's hump.

The whale arched its back and slid under the surface with Firebeard hooked fast. Little Dan had no way of hanging on and was swept away never to be seen again.

When the whale surfaced again, Firebeard was nowhere to be seen. Had he perished in the water? Drowned in his quest for gold?

No, he was very much alive. He had climbed down the whale's blow hole, breathing the air the whale had drawn in through the large opening at the back of its head.

Suddenly, there was a great gush as the whale opened the flap on his blow hole to release the air. Pop! Out blew Firebeard, hurled into the sky on a fountain of water. He landed with a thud and quickly clambered back inside the hole, ready for the next dive.

Firebeard survived like this for another 2 weeks. Two hours under water and one on the surface, breathing whale breath then fresh air.

Then one morning after a particularly long dive and powerful ejection, Firebeard saw land. It was a wonderful sight which brought a smile to his battered face.

The whale had swam all the way to England and had entered the Bristol channel. It was as if he knew where his passenger needed to go.

King Celery

Captain Celery's journey home was less eventful. With a light ship, a healthy crew and plenty to eat and drink, it was more like a cruise. The men sang every night as they snacked on celery(the vegetable, not the man).

To pass the time, the crew would race against the dolphins as they swam alongside the ship.

The chef organised celery swallowing contests to see who could shove the longest stick down their throats without choking.

All the time, they kept their eyes peeled for the Black Oyster but it was nowhere to be seen.

Eventually, the Happy Goose arrived safely home in Bristol.

As they docked in the harbour, crowds turned out in anticipation of seeing the mountain of gold Celery had brought home.

Confused and disappointed they watched as Captain Celery unloaded his vegetables.

"Where's the gold? Where's Firebeard?" they shouted.

They had all expected the legendary Firebeard to arrive home first, but it was stick man with a load of vegetables!

"What's that green stuff?" they roared.

Captain Celery leapt ashore and addressed the crowd:

"Firebeard is history," he said and then, waving a stick of celery above his head, declared:

"And this, my friends, is the future."

Celery's crew threw sticks of celery into the crowd. Cautiously, some of the onlookers nibbled on the stalks. Then more joined in until the entire crowd was munching noisily in delight.

Celery – both the man and the vegetable – was a big hit and soon orders to buy more were flooding in. Within the hour, he had sold half the celery and news arrived that King Charles II, King of England, had reserved the other half and had sent an army to collect it.

Because Captain Celery was smarter than your average pirate, he had also brought home a few live plants which he set about planting to harvest next year.

His trip had been a fantastic success. He had earned lots of money and was guaranteed more every year when the next crop of celery was ripe.

He had of course doubled crossed Captain Firebeard, but he would be causing no trouble because he had probably drowned.

Firebeard Returns

After the excitement of the celery, the dock fell quiet for the evening. The sun was sinking behind the horizon and all was calm.

Then the peace was shattered by the most almighty crash as Captain Firebeard dropped from the sky in a plume of water. He crashed through the rigging of the Happy Goose and landed in an undignified heap on the deck.

Captain Celery and his crew stood motionless with their mouths open in shock.

Firebeard staggered to his feet (well, his foot actually), spat out a gallon of sea water and brushed down his clothes.

"Well, Celery you two-faced, lily-livered scoundrel. I'm back for my revenge."

Firebeard drew his sword and before Celery could snap out of his state of shock, took a huge swing at him, slashing the pirate across the chest.

Celery had no sword so, quick as a flash, he reached for a stick of celery and threw it hard in the direction of Captain Firebeard.

The celery whipped him across the cheek with a loud slap. Then another stick came flying across and hit Firebeard's face with a thwack.

Firebeard staggered backwards and was caught by a third stick right in the eye. He wobbled, tottered and fell back over the side of the ship.

Splosh! Firebeard hit the water with a huge splash. He thrashed around, gulping for air, but the weight of his iron claw and sword pulled him down, deep into the harbour.

A few bubbles rose to the surface, then an eerie silence descended. He was gone. The most fearsome pirate that ever lived, lived no more.

Later that evening, Captain Celery was taking in the peace of the moonlight as it cast its silvery light across the sea. A few gulls circled overhead and on the horizon a whale broke the surface, its huge back casting a shadow against the sky.

Celery squinted into the distance trying to make sense of what he saw.

It was the shape of a rather large man held aloft by a jet of water…

The End

About the Author

Nick Band has spent most
of his life telling stories as
a journalist, public relations
professional and a father.

His greatest story-telling
achievement was an epic
improvised story session for
his young son which lasted
an exhausting seven years!

Nick was born in Devon but
moved to London and then
Berkshire where he now lives
with his wife Gabby and
children Milo and Ella.

Captain Celery is his first
children's book.

About the Artist

Sian is a professional artist.
She learnt to paint at Central
Saint Martins in London.

Her favourite pictures are
doodles on the back of
envelopes. You don't need
canvases to create
masterpieces!

She loves walking her smelly
dog Cadbury in Windsor
Great Park where she gets
ideas for new paintings.

Sian lives near the Thames
in an old house with her
husband Rob and daughters
Trixie, Scarlet and Marina.

Printed in Great Britain
by Amazon

45051221П00028